The Adventures of Duke and Daisy:

Daisy Comes Home

Story by
Robin & Logan Nieto
Illustrations by
Ellie Lieberman

A Pipe & Thimble Publishing Book
24830 Narbonne Ave
Lomita, CA 90717

First edition.

Original Illustrations by Ellie Lieberman
www.ellielieberman.weebly.com
Copyright © 2016. All Rights Reserved.
Used by permission.

ISBN-13: 978-0692915189

ISBN-10: 0692915184

Other books by Robin Nieto:

Tales from Mema's Garden:
Monarch Butterflies

Tales from Mema's Garden: Spiders

This is dedicated to the two sweet, sweet, sweet fur babies who inspired the story and the series!

It was a beautiful and uneventful day at the house. Birds were chirping, the sun was shining, and Duke was sleeping soundly on the couch. He lived in a single-dog home, which he was very pleased with. His humans loved him very much, and he adored them just the same.

Most of Duke's afternoons were spent lounging on his blanket daydreaming about cookies, going to the dog park to play, or going for rides in the car. Duke was spoiled and liked it that way; he even had special homemade treats baked just for him. All was perfect, but Duke had no idea that on this beautiful day... that would all change.

There was a knock at the door and a somewhat unfamiliar scent for Duke. Dad gave him a few extra minutes to sniff at the bottom of the door, but he just tilted his head in confusion. Suddenly, the door opened. Mom was standing there... but what was she holding? It was small, fuzzy, different colors, and made strange noises. Duke was curious.

"It" was then placed on the floor in "Duke's" house. What was going on? Was "it" visiting? "It" couldn't be staying? What was "it"?

At this point, Duke was very confused and heard his humans calling it "Daisy". What is a Daisy? Why is it here in my house? Duke noticed Daisy had a tail like him, a nose like him, and ears like him, but was definitely different than him.

Within a couple of minutes, "Daisy" was running around the living room chasing her tail, something Duke would never even consider doing. This was certainly annoying.

Daisy appeared to be tiring out and did not seem to be leaving yet. Duke found his comfy spot on the couch right in the middle of his favorite blanket. He was very tired and began closing his eyes when, suddenly, he felt a thump right next to him. He opened his eyes only to see Daisy joining him on his blanket.

Duke decided it was time to let this Daisy know how things work in his house, so he growled at her. She responded simply by tilting her head and letting out the most pathetic bark he had ever heard. The only problem was, she didn't move. This was his couch and he wasn't going to budge... even if it meant sleeping next to her.

Hours went by and neither one of them had stirred. As a matter of fact, Daisy was snoring. Before they even realized it, morning had come.

Duke opened his eyes, let out a yawn, and looked to his left expecting to see the fuzzy intruder still there. To his surprise, it wasn't. Where had it gone? Did it finally leave?

"Bark!"

Nope... it was still here, and it was crying and whining at the back door. This was where the humans let Duke outside to go potty, and now it seemed this thing wanted to go potty, too.

The humans were still sleeping, and Daisy didn't seem to be letting up. Duke didn't know what to do, because he hadn't had to use the potty this early since he was a puppy.... A puppy... That's it! Daisy was a puppy!

At this point, it looked like Daisy might be staying for a while. Duke decided he was going to teach her a thing or two. This would be, of course, to make his own life a little easier.

Daisy continued barking and whining at the back door. Duke decided that this was the perfect teaching opportunity. Daisy needed to learn how to go outside. He bolted from the back door to the stairs, with Daisy close behind.

When reaching the top of the steps, he realized she had disappeared. His heart sank. Then, suddenly, he heard that familiar whine at the bottom of the stairs. Duke ran down to the bottom in a panic. Daisy looked terrified and was shaking. She had never encountered a challenge like this.

Time was running out, and Duke knew something had to be done and quick. He began running up and down the first couple steps, trying to show Daisy that she could do it. He also began barking for encouragement. After a few moments, Daisy gathered her courage and went up to the first step. At this point, Dad appeared at the top and that was all the motivation she needed to go all the way, with Duke close behind.

Dad saw the urgency in the situation and ran down the stairs with Duke on his heels. Daisy, on the other hand, now had issues with going down. They both waited at the bottom for a moment, and Daisy let out a big howl. Finally, she ran down the steps and, with a slight tumble, made it to the bottom.

Now all three, Dad, Duke, and Daisy ran for the back door. It opened and Duke ran out. He immediately turned to see that Daisy had once again had disappeared.

Running back inside for fear that something has happened to her, Duke saw Daisy sitting next to a puddle. She looked ashamed. Duke knew that feeling from when he was a puppy. He knew exactly what would cheer her up... a toy. They began playing tug o' war with an unstuffed striped zebra, really a sad sight to see.

When playtime was finally over, both Duke and Daisy were completely tuckered out. They both hopped on the couch and cuddled up in their own favorite blanket. As Daisy began to doze off, Duke gave her a small lick on the face, letting his little sister know that she will get it next time.

Robin Nieto is a Southern California native, wife, mother of four, adopted mother of five fur babies, and MiMi to three rambunctious boys. Robin is a long-time friend of Elaine MacInnes, and co-author of the Tales from Mema's Garden series with her. She is also the author of The Adventures of Duke and Daisy series, the upcoming How I Fought Like A Girl, co-author with her daughter, Kindra Sowder, on Paper People Glass Houses, and the contributing author to Beyond The Fairy Door Anthology.

Facebook: robinmnieto

Logan Nieto is a high school student, poet, and an editor for the Torrance High School Torch. He has a passion for dogs, video games, and pickles.
This is his first book, but not his last.

Made in the USA
San Bernardino, CA
04 July 2017